This book belongs to:

_____

Loving Family

Home for the Holidays

Written by Colleen Tomasso
Illustrated by Joy Allen

"Jingle bells, jingle bells, Santa's on his way," sings Sister.
"Can we show Baby how our family gets ready for Christmas?"

"That's a nice idea," says Mom.
"Which holiday traditions should we share?"

"I know! We can decorate cookies for Santa," Sister says.
"Baby can help me with the star cookie."

Silly Baby! Silly Jingles!

Dad asks, "What else can we show Baby?"

"I know! We can decorate the tree!" says Sister, standing on her tippy toes. "This one says, My First Christmas."

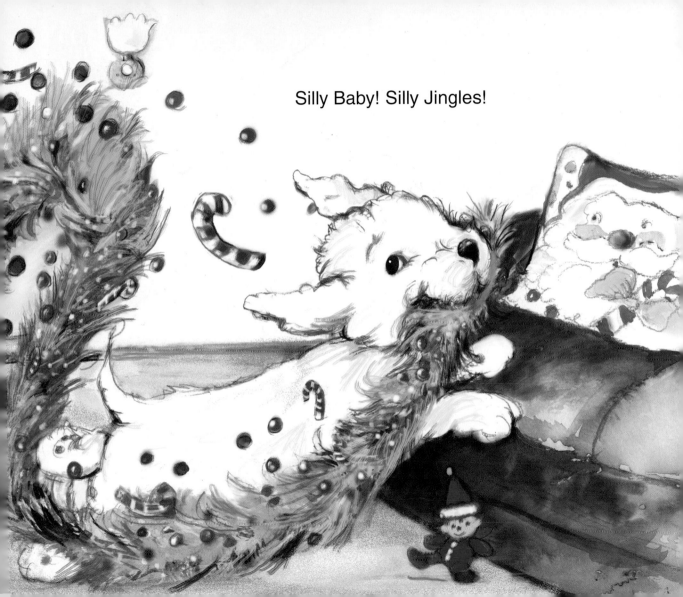

Silly Baby! Silly Jingles!

"Something's missing. Daddy, will you help me?" asks Sister. "Look, Baby, I'm putting this star on top of the tree!"

Sister runs upstairs to Mom and Dad's bedroom. "Let's wrap some presents."

She wraps and ties and tapes all the pretty presents. "This one is for someone I love...no peeking!"

Silly Baby! Silly Jingles!

What a mess! Looks like it's time for a bath.

"Scrub-a-dub-dub, put Jingles in the tub!" sings Sister.

"OOPS!"
Sister accidentally bumps the
bottle of bubbles into the bath!

Sister calls out, "Oh no, Jingles, where are you going?"
"Follow those bubbles!" says Dad.

Is Jingles in the nursery? "I see
Baby's crib, but I don't see Jingles." says Sister.

Is Jingles in Sister's bedroom?
"I see my quilt, but I don't see Jingles."

Is Jingles in the attic?
"I see boxes, but I don't see Jingles."

Is Jingles in the front yard?
"I see a snowman, but I don't see Jingles."

Is Jingles near the Christmas tree?
"I see cookie crumbs and paw prints,
but I don't see Jingles."

"There's Jingles! He opened all the presents from Mommy and Daddy!" says Sister. "Christmas pajamas for everyone, even Jingles!"

*"Woof!
Woof!"*

What a wonderful day of sharing Christmas traditions with The Loving Family. Mom, Dad, Sister, and Baby gather near the tree to sing a special song.

"Jingle bells, jingle bells, Jingles likes to play! Oh what fun it is to play around the house all day. Hey!"